The Brave Strong Mermaid

by Hilary Moore
Illustrated by Catty Flores

*Dedicated to all the girls around the world
who like to say what they think!*

Diversity ✧
Publishing

© Hilary Moore 2015 www.bravestronggirls.com

Illustrations by Catty Flores © 2015 www.cattyflores.com

Published by:

Diversity Publishing
Diversity Publishing is a trade name of Brave Strong Books Ltd
28A Springfield
WD231GL
Bushey Heath
Herts
United Kingdom
www.bravestronggirls.com

nce upon a time, there was a brave, strong mermaid called Allona. Full of joy and courage, her greatest delight was to explore the oceans and discover new wonders. She loved to race and leap through the sparkling waters of the world with her best friend, Nerissa. During storms, they would call to each other when they found struggling ships and rescue anyone thrown into the water by the crashing waves.

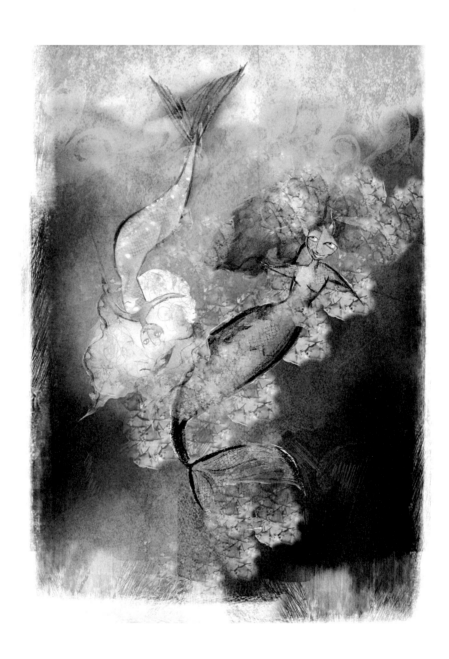

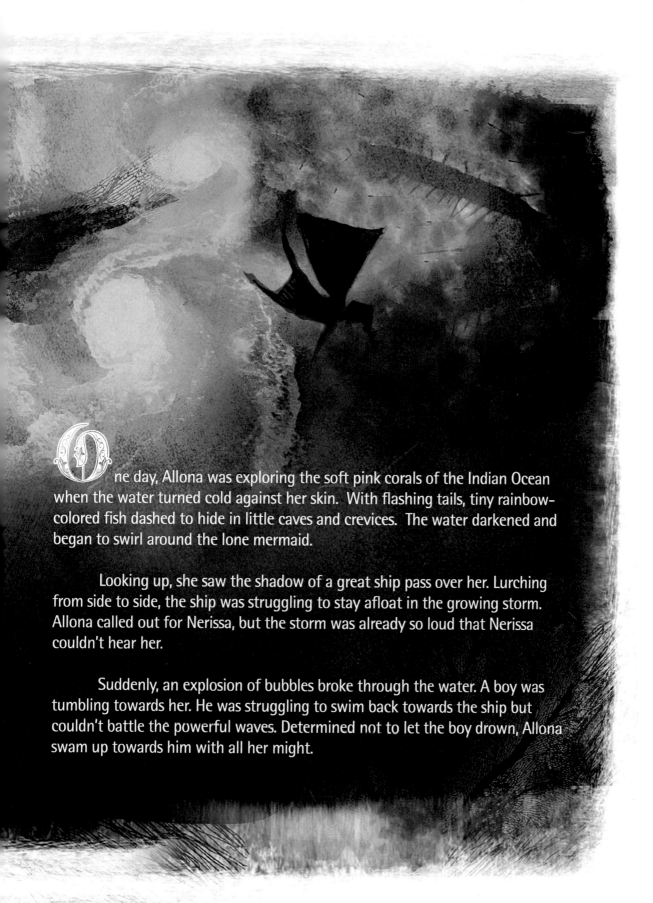

One day, Allona was exploring the soft pink corals of the Indian Ocean when the water turned cold against her skin. With flashing tails, tiny rainbow-colored fish dashed to hide in little caves and crevices. The water darkened and began to swirl around the lone mermaid.

Looking up, she saw the shadow of a great ship pass over her. Lurching from side to side, the ship was struggling to stay afloat in the growing storm. Allona called out for Nerissa, but the storm was already so loud that Nerissa couldn't hear her.

Suddenly, an explosion of bubbles broke through the water. A boy was tumbling towards her. He was struggling to swim back towards the ship but couldn't battle the powerful waves. Determined not to let the boy drown, Allona swam up towards him with all her might.

She pulled the boy into her arms and kicked her powerful tail towards the surface. As she broke through to the cold night air, she saw the ship already far away, tumbling and rocking through the stormy waters.

The mountainous waves rushed surging and crashing around the mermaid and the boy. The thunderous clouds rolled darkly above them. This was one of the biggest storms Allona had ever seen but she was determined that somehow she would get the drowning boy to dry land.

Fighting against the surging waves, Allona swam with him in her arms until, escaping the storm, they arrived at a sandy beach. Overjoyed but exhausted, they both fell asleep, with Allona's tail in the water and her head resting on the sand.

In the morning, as the pale gold sun rose on the horizon, the boy stirred. He gasped in amazement when he saw the mermaid. Allona, waking, quickly turned to swim for open sea.

The boy called out to her. "Brave mermaid, won't you stay and tell me your name?"

"I am Allona", she answered and then laughed. "I bet I am the first mermaid you have ever seen!" She leapt out of the water, and flipped her tail over her head. The scales on her tail glimmered in the sunshine, splashing diamond droplets of water into the air.

He laughed too. "It is wonderful to meet you. My name is Prince Ranesh." The boy had beautiful chocolate-colored eyes and a gentle smile.

"A prince! I have never met a human prince before. You had better head back to your kingdom - and I, to my home." Allona swam a little further out but Ranesh cried out to her once more.

"I don't want you to leave me. You are so brave, and such fun. Please – I will do anything to stay with you."

Allona looked at the boy. "But you can't possibly play with me in the sea with those silly legs – you would need a tail!"

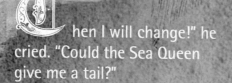

hen I will change!" he cried. "Could the Sea Queen give me a tail?"

The Sea Queen was a formidable woman, but Allona was willing to try. "It is possible" she said. "But I shall have to carry you in my arms – it is many, many miles from here."

Together, they swam through the Indian Ocean and then into the frozen waters where the Sea Queen lived. A ring of sharks guarded the Sea Queen's palace. The sharks eyed them suspiciously, but allowed them to pass. Angel fish – sparkling icy blue and silver – surrounded them and guided them into the palace.

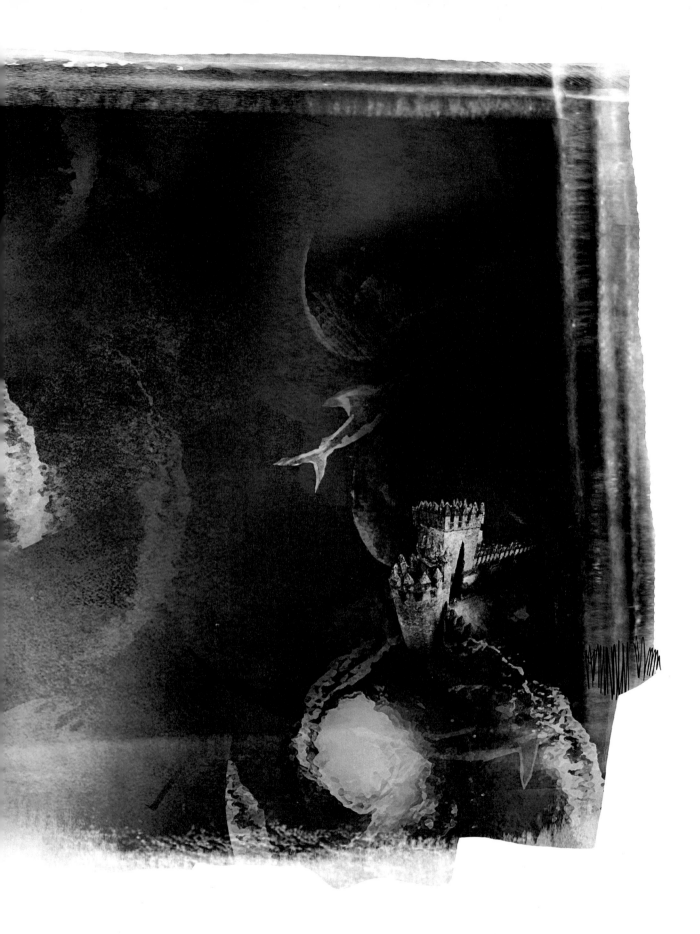

The Sea Queen was sitting on a throne of ice in a huge watery hall seething with great whales. At first, she was furious that Allona had brought a human to see her, but when Prince Ranesh begged the Queen to give him a tail, she finally agreed. For this favor, she demanded a very high price. *For as long as Prince Ranesh had a tail, Allona would lose her voice.*

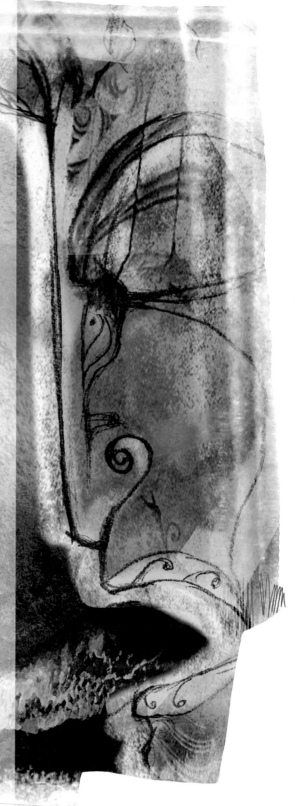

Allona loved being with Ranesh, but it was certainly not worth losing her voice for! She gripped him by the arm to tell him to refuse, but before she could stop him, Ranesh had agreed!

The Angel fish surrounded the boy until his whole body was a whirlwind of silver and blue. The Sea Queen chanted a spell and when the Angel fish moved away, Ranesh's legs had turned into a strong, scaly tail. He turned to Allona, smiling in triumph. Outraged, she tried to shout at him, but no sound came out.

Turning from Ranesh, Allona swam as fast as she could out of the palace and back towards her home. As soon as she found Nerissa, Allona explained what had happened by tracing words in the seabed. They knew they must take action.

Nerissa used a giant sea shell to call a special meeting of all the mermaids. Together, they decided they must find Ranesh and persuade him to change back.

They spread out through the ocean and it was Nerissa who finally found him just beyond the Sea Queen's palace. He was practicing swimming with his new tail, but also looked a little lonely. When she called, all the other mermaids – including Allona – came to encircle Ranesh.

They angrily told him that he must return Allona's voice – even if it meant him leaving the sea forever. The mermaids needed their voices to call for rescue teams to help drowning humans during a storm. Did princesses in his kingdom lose their voices just because princes wanted them to? That wasn't how things worked for the mermaids!

Ranesh began to protest, but when he saw Allona's unhappiness, he understood what a terrible mistake he had made. He agreed to give up his tail.

In exchange for reversing her spell, the Sea Queen made Ranesh promise to throw a flower into the sea once a year to show that he had not forgotten his time in the oceans.

Allona and Nerissa carried him one last time to the sandy beach in his kingdom. Giving him a string of beautiful shells to remember them by, they promised to keep rescuing his people from drowning.

Ranesh stood staring out to sea as Allona and Nerissa disappeared together, their green tails dancing and sparkling in the blue water. He smiled a tearful smile, then turned towards his kingdom – into the joyful arms of his parents, the King and Queen.

E very year after that, he came to the sandy beach and threw
flowers into the sea – one for every life Allona and Nerissa had saved
that year, and one to show that he remembered his time in the ocean.

Ranesh would stand on the beach thinking of Allona. He was
a fine prince, and the kingdom needed him, but he had never found
as strong or as special a princess as Allona. Sometimes Allona would
come on the same day as Ranesh just to see that he was well. The
brave mermaid would always hide behind a rock, in case the sight of
her tempted him back into the sea.

HILARY MOORE

Hilary is a busy mom who works in international business.
She has a PhD and MBA and has published several books.

Most importantly, she is mother of five-year-old Iona - a girl
she hopes will grow up brave and strong, inspired by great girl role models in the books she reads. There aren't many of those great role models in traditional fairy tales, so Hilary decided
to write some!

100% of the profits from the 'Brave Strong Girls' go to charities that help to educate and empower girls around the world.

CATTY FLORES

Catty was born in Paris but moved to Spain when her family decided to return home. At an early age she began exploring the art of playing with water, pencils, hands and colours. Catty loved
to redecorate and filled every space she could reach. Needless
to say, her family was horrified.

Fortunately, this mischievousness gave back lots of challenges and satisfaction over the years. The most recent one has been working on the Brave, Strong Girls series, a beautiful opportunity to help overcome stereotypes and preconceptions."

Catty's artistic playmates have included international publishing houses and advertising agencies like M&C Saatchi London, Gruner Jahr Mondadori and Helbling Languages.
www.cattyflores.com

The 'Brave Strong Girls' concept

100% of the profits from the 'Brave Strong Girls' series will
go to charities that help to educate and empower girls around the world.

The Brave, Strong Girls series is specially created to give children strong girl role models in the books they read, with female characters who are resilient, who are brave, and who think for themselves. Fairy tales have a wonderful place in young children's lives – sparking their imagination and teaching them about life. Unfortunately, the traditional versions are unfair to girls and women. Almost all the evil characters are older women, jealous of their younger counterparts. The young girl characters are often judged only on their beauty. They also spend much of their time totally passive – asleep, trapped, or helpless victims. They make silly mistakes and their only chance of a happy ending is to be rescued by, or married to, a prince.

We know this does not reflect reality, and the Brave, Strong Girls Series is putting this right! It's a series for girls and boys - both gain a lot from seeing female characters they can respect. The books are fun and beautifully illustrated. They keep the magic and beauty of the traditional fairytales, while also sending much better messages about the amazing talents and courage of girls and women.

Other books in the series:

Brave Strong Snow White and the Seven Dwarfs
Brave Strong Leonie and the Race of a Lifetime

Made in the USA
San Bernardino, CA
29 December 2015